To Judith —
May "Trouble" never
find you !

Sheila Numan
June, 2009

About the Creator

Kendra Duncan is a very creative, thirteen year old girl, who loves helping people and making them smile. One night, while watching the St. Jude Telethon, Kendra decided that she'd like to do something to help children afflicted with cancer. Soon after, the entire concept of Trouble was "born" and the rest is history.

About the Author

Sheila Duncan is the wind behind Trouble's back - making sure everyone knows about him and benefits from the wonderful soothing influence he seems to have on kids and adults alike.

About the Illustrator

Annette Nicolas is the illustrator who took Kendra's original sketches of Trouble, Nonnie, Roxy and Luigi and brought them to life, creating a world in which they could learn and love and share some magic with our readers.

Trouble's Supporters

Throughout this journey Trouble has had many helpful friends along the way. We are grateful to you all for your never ending help and guidance and we thank you: Michael Kuber, Annette Nicolas, Judy and Steve Howe, Edie Lewis, Elizabeth Hunt, Claire Roche, Bob and Deb Zarelli, Jeannine Camarda, Jack Schylling, Deborah DeSantis, Barbara Vaughn, Susan Donahue, Ivy Lane, Jack McHugh, Judson Percy, Roberta Chadis, Phyllis McGinness, Phyllis Karas, Carol Jendresak, Linda Dearborne, Dan Hurley, Howard Stubblefield and The Seminara Family.

The following are Trademarks of Larkin Ltd.

"Trouble"
"Here's Trouble"
"Where There's Trouble, There's Hope"
"When Trouble Comes, You're Never Alone"

Published by Larkin, Ltd.
P.O. Box 952
Marblehead, MA 01945

781-631-0887
Fax: 781-631-0883
trouble@troublesaysbetough.com
www.troublesaysbetough.com

ISBN-13: 978-0-615-13564-9
ISBN-10: 0-615-13564-1

DEDICATION

Kendra and I would like to dedicate our
first Trouble book to her mother, my sister,
Sharon Duncan. Sharon has been a source of
inspiration and encouragement from the very
beginning ... and we love her for it!

Late at night, in a dark alley in New York City, someone left a cardboard box marked "FRAGILE". There the box sat with the barrels of trash and a few nibbling rats. But this box marked "FRAGILE" was not filled with trash. It was filled with – puppies! Tan pups and brown pups and one frisky gray pup with a black spot around his eye. His name was Trouble.

Someone had left the puppies there hoping they would be safe until they found good homes. They had even taken the time to leave a note with the puppies' names. But for now, Trouble and his siblings were on their own! The stray pups searched everywhere for food and scraps and hoped strangers would be kind. Trouble managed to stay busy during the day. He played hide-and-seek with his brothers and sisters and enjoyed the bones he found in the alley; but at night, he dreamed of a warm bed and a loving hand to pat his head.

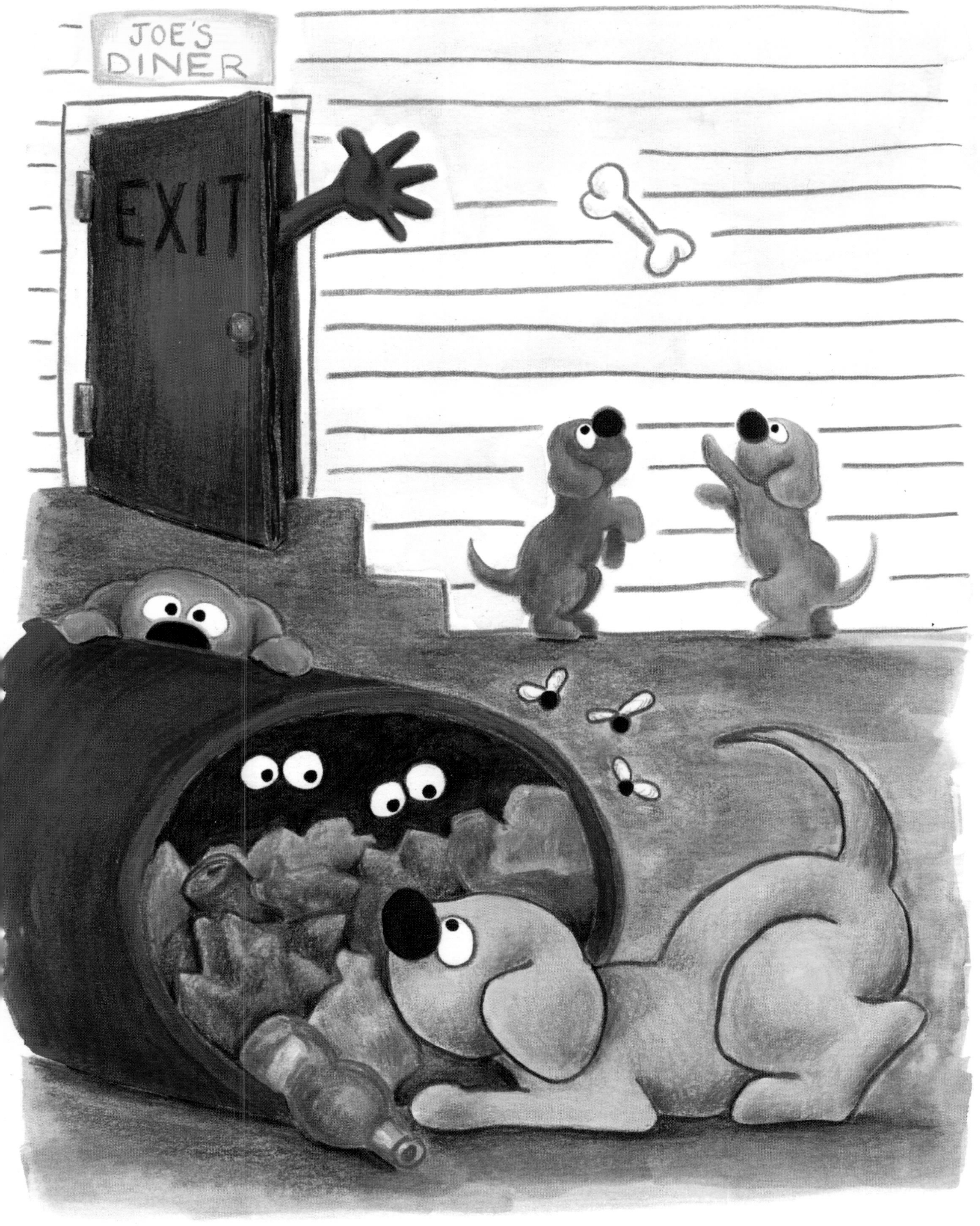
JOE'S
DINER
EXIT

It was hard and dangerous living on the streets. One by one Trouble's siblings scampered off on their own adventures, leaving Trouble to spend many nights cold and alone. He spent many days tired and hungry. He was losing hope. Trouble needed help. He soon found it at Nonnie's Pizza Shop.

Nonnie owned the pizza shop and she loved dogs. She saw that Trouble was tired and hungry. She wanted to keep him safe. She brought him right into her home and adopted him as her very own pup.

Nonnie taught Trouble that he needed to be a good pup and stay away from danger. She also told him there might be some difficult days – he might not feel well, or he might have a problem with another dog or he might not be paying attention like he should. But whatever happened, Nonnie always told Trouble to "be tough" and take care of himself – just like he did when he was a pup in the alley. And that he should always have hope that good things were coming!

Soon, Nonnie adopted another dog, a Golden Retriever named Roxy. Trouble was now a big brother! Both Trouble and Nonnie taught Roxy to be a good pup. They also taught her to "be tough" and take care of herself. This meant listening to Nonnie and paying attention and staying away from danger.

When Nonnie got older, she sold the pizza shop. Now she could spend all of her time with Trouble and Roxy.

The three of them had lots of fun. They took long walks and had picnics and played catch. Trouble and Roxy loved Nonnie and she took very good care of them, but Nonnie wanted to be sure they could take care of themselves and each other when she wasn't there. While most of their days were filled with fun and games, they also had to listen and follow the rules so that they would be safe - just like when they were crossing a very busy street.

One day, while Nonnie was out shopping and Trouble was home with Roxy, he looked out the window and saw a little dog running in the street. The little dog looked scared and lost. A big truck was coming up behind the little dog and the driver couldn't see him. Trouble woofed to the little dog but he couldn't hear Trouble's warning bark.

Trouble ran down the stairs, out the door and woofed again, "Get on the sidewalk!" The little dog heard him and jumped up on the sidewalk just as the big truck zoomed by him. The poor little dog was shaking – and dirty!

Trouble and Roxy took the
little dog inside and gave
him a nice warm bath.
When Nonnie came home,
she named him "Luigi" and
said he could stay with them.

Trouble and Roxy were delighted to have a new brother. But, they sure had their work to do teaching Luigi to "be tough" and take care of himself. Until now, he hadn't been doing a very good job! But those were lessons for another day. Today was over and the three of them curled up together to sleep. Nonnie read them a magical bedtime story. As Trouble dozed off, he started dreaming about how he could help people and dogs have hope, be tough and be loved, just as Nonnie had helped him. Maybe he could work in a little magic too!

But there was something
about Luigi ....